TROBO and The Shape Shifting Shoebox

in

"Snot Shot"

Written by Chris Harden

"TROBO and The Shape Shifting Shoebox in Snot Shot"

Written by Chris Harden

Dedicated to Laurie, Asher, and Finley.
You will always be my inspiration.

Table of Contents:

Table of Contents: 3

Stuck 4

Corugami School...7

Shape Shifting What?..................................14

The Library, Sort Of...................................29

The Comlok...40

Playing Hooky 46

Homework Stinks 57

Pop Pop Fizz Quiz.......................................70

The Baby Sitter 77

It's All In the Numbers 83

By Rhino, I Think I've Got It!....................94

Shoe and Tell...97

The Snot Shot...102

Making the Grade.......................................117

About TROBOs...120

Thank You...126

Stuck

SPLAT!! Newton is hit by a huge blog of goo. He is slammed against the wall. It hurts just a little. He's coated. He's stuck! The giant snot ball has plastered him to the chalk board. He feels like a flat piece of gum pushed under someone's desk. And he's dripping.

Around the room, other TROBO children are running, hiding, or ducking from a large cannon with a pig nose. The device is made of cardboard. It sits on top of a wheel like a unicycle. It spins around in circles, shooting green, liquid goo at everything. Each time it shoots, it rolls back a little. It refills and fires again. Each time it fires, it sounds like a giant, roly-poly sneezing pig. Kids are screaming. The pig nose is squealing and sneezing.

"Help!"

"SNORT-SQUEEL -SPLAT!"

"Yuk! That was my favorite t-shirt!"

"No don't point this way!"

"SNORT-SQUEEL -SPLOOP!"

"Ewwww!!! It got in my mouth!"

"NewTON!!!! I knew I should not have let you bring that thing in here! I'll see to it that you never get out of this grade, if you don't do something NOW!" Newton's teacher, Dr. Braun screams from across the room. He's too late to duck the pig nose and SPLOOCH! He gets a watermelon-sized lugee right in the ear. "Ack!" he screams. Lugees are snot balls.

Ok that was awesome, Newton thinks, but he dares not show a grin. As much as Newton doesn't like school, he does not want to make it worse by laughing at the teacher.

He looks around the room. His pig nose is making a drippy mess of everything. He's got to do something fast. He sees his twin sister, Curie running and ducking under a desk. She dodges the last snotty cannon ball. It squirts another oozy blob right next to him.

He remembers how he got to this point...

Corugami School

Corugami School for Exceptional Robots

One week earlier...

Newton scarfs down a few last bites of breakfast as he is nearly yanked out of his chair by his mom.

"Hurry or you will be late for your first day," she says in a flustered tone. Mom loves him, but Newton can be the type to drag his feet when he doesn't want to do something.

Today is one of those days. Newton does not want to go to a new school. He doesn't even want to go to his old school. But a new school? New friends? New teachers? New homework? Ugh… new homework. Newton is convinced that nobody likes homework. Not even geeks and teachers' pets. *Why do schools even exist?* He grabs one last scoop of cereal from the bowl before tossing the spoon back in. It makes a "bloop" sound as the milk scatters out and then swallows the spoon.

Newton yawns as he plops into the back seat of Dad's car. Curie is there. She's ecstatic at the idea of this new school for the "exceptional TROBOs".

What does exceptional mean, anyways? Newton wonders. It sounds like they won a prize, like a one week vacation to somewhere cool. But it's not. It's school. Just fancy school.

He doesn't think much more about it. He looks out the window as Dad drives. Their house shrinks into the distance. The day is beautiful. He sticks his hand out the window for fun. The wind feels good. The window rolls up and nearly catches Newton's hand, before he yanks it in. "Hey!" he glares at Dad. Dad looks back, "Oh sorry buddy, I want to talk to you guys."

Oh boy thinks Newton, *here it comes. The new school pep talk.*

"I'm so proud of both of you, and I know you are going to like this school. I know we've moved a few times because of Mommy and Daddy's work, but we're going to be here a while…" Newton's

dad begins. "This school is different. It's a special school where they are going to teach you stuff other schools don't…" *blah blah blah,* Newton drifts off. He doesn't have much of an attention span and so he never catches most of what Dad says. It's nothing personal. Dad just happens to talk a lot.

A little while later, Dad, Newton and Curie arrive at the school. The school signs says, "Corugami School for Exceptional Robots."

"Cool," says Curie, as she grabs Dad's hand. "Whatever," says Newton. He walks a couple feet behind Dad and Sister dreading every step. His shoes feel like the laces have been replaced with heavy chains dipped in dread.

They get to the first classroom. Dad introduces himself to the teacher. The teacher is a round, potbellied adult TROBO with a bushy, black mustache and matching set of eyebrows. Newton thinks he looks like he scowls more than he smiles.

"Hi, I'm Dr. Braun," the teacher says in a gruff voice and shakes Dad's hand.

"Hi, I'm Magnes, and this is Curie." Dad points to Curie, who beams at the teacher. Dr. Braun smiles back, "It's lovely to meet you, Curie."

"Thank you," she replies, gleaming. *Already working as teacher's pet,* Newton thinks.

"And this is Newton," Dad points to Newton. Newton looks straight faced at the new teacher. Dr. Braun's eyes show that they detect a bit of attitude from Newton. "Hello, Newton, it's nice to meet you too," Dr. Braun says.

"Yeah, thanks," Newton replies. He and Dr. Braun look at each other a moment. Dr. Braun can tell Newton is going to be a "challenging student".

"Well children, let's get settled in. You can pick a couple of seats as you like," Dr. Braun says. Dad hugs the kids and leaves. When he hugs Newton, he says, "You're gonna love it here, I promise."

Newton is not so sure.

They pick seats near the back. Curie wants to sit up front, but Newton never sits up there. "I can see better from back here," he insists. Her bond with him is stronger than her need to sit in the front row, so she joins him. But Newton doesn't stay comfortable for long.

13

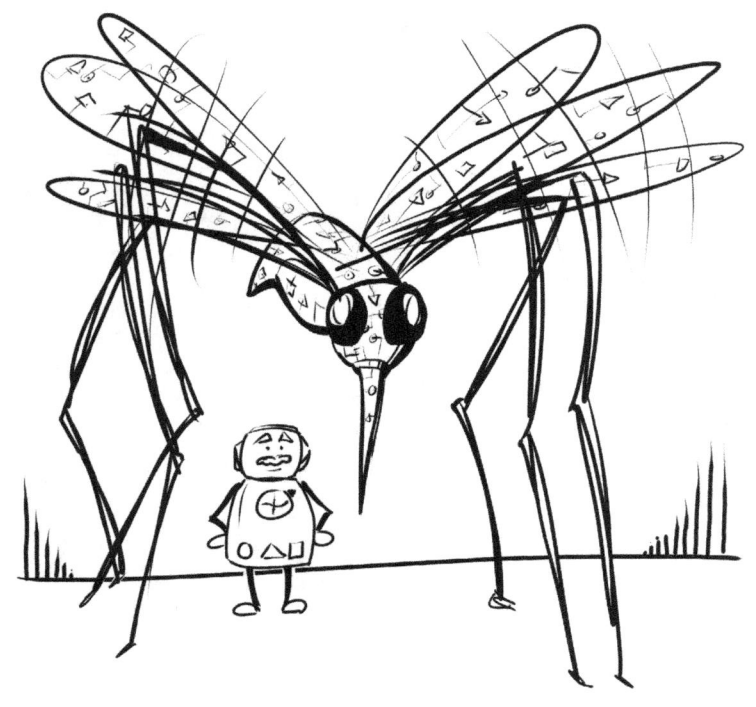

Shape Shifting What?

Soon the bell rings. All the kids are out of their

seats, running and making noise. Dr. Braun tells

everyone to settle down. No one listens.

He raises his voice. No luck.

BWAAAAAAAAAAAAAAAAAAAMPPPPP!!!!!!

A loud horn sound fills the room, and everyone freezes. They look at Dr. Braun, who holds an air horn high up in his hand. He stands there in silence for a moment, looking everyone over. Stone. Faced.

"Oh I'm so glad to have your attention. Please sit down now," he smiles. There is a little rustling and everyone settles down.

Newton flashes a questioning look over at Curie, who is grinning ear to ear. She's excited by the new teacher's loud horn approach to getting everyone's attention.

"Everyone, I'd like to welcome you to the Corugami School for Exceptional Robots. This is a very special magnet school that most TROBOs will never see. Only a select few will enter these great halls, and even fewer will graduate from here. It is a fine institution…" he goes on and on.

Sounds like dad, Newton thinks and drifts out for a bit, looking around the room. He sees other boy and girl TROBOs of all shapes and sizes. Some look smarter than others. Some look tired. Some look hungry. Some of the girls are pretty.

"…and that brings me to why we will start teaching you this very basic skill today. With it, you will go on to do amazing work with the human children." Newton comes back to listening to Dr. Braun. His interest perks a bit.

The human children? he thinks. *What did I miss?*

"If you do well, you will be invited to try out for HPS. That stands for Human Protection Service. HPS is an elite force of TROBOs that, among other things, protect the human race from losing all of their knowledge."

"What?" Newton blurts out loud.

Dr. Braun stops talking and looks over at Newton a minute. He is surprised and bothered to be interrupted. Curie asks, "He means, why are they losing their knowledge?"

"Good question, Curie," Dr. Braun answers. "But that discussion is for another time." He looks back over at Newton. Newton shrugs and forces a weak smile.

"Where was I... Oh yes, uh, so... work hard, and just maybe, you'll be accepted into HPS someday. For now, you must practice the basics to even have a chance," Dr. Braun continues.

Dr. Braun tells them to get the book from under their desks. Surprised he hadn't noticed it before, Newton looks under his desk. The book is ENORMOUS in size! It weighs more than he does. Each TROBO struggles to get the book moved and on top of their desk. Some books are dropped and crush toes – "Ow! Poor little piggie". Some pinch fingers – "Aiee! That was my GOOD thumb." One TROBO gets stuck under her book – "Help! It's crushing my liver!" she squeals.

Dr. Braun squeaks, rushes over, and helps her out from under it and waits for the room to settle. "Everyone, I'd like to welcome you to Shape Shifting Class". A murmur starts over the class. Newton and Curie exchange glances – "shape shifting? What's that?" Other TROBOs are asking around. Whispers fly around the room.

"Sounds like geometry," says one kid.

"Sounds like a sculpting class," replies another.

"Is it a baking class? Like when you sift flour to make biscuits?" one asks. Her stomach growls.

"Shape SHIFTING, not SIFTING," replies another.

"Oh."

Newton looks down at the cover of the book, it reads, "Shoebox Shape Shifting 101. Edition 1032.

Centuries of finely tuned shoebox combinations collected in one titanic tome." It is a hardback book and bound with leather.

"It definitely feels titanic," says Newton to Curie.

She's not listening. She's giddy and already flipping through the pages. Flip. Flip. Flipping. Oohing and Ahhing. Newton can tell Curie is quite excited. She's tapping her feet quickly on the floor.

Although they are twins, Newton and Curie are quite different. Curie's pink, purple, and green colors don't match anything in Newton's red, yellow, and blue colors. All the TROBOs have multiple colors on their bodies. Newton and Curie happen to be grey, like their mom and dad, but other TROBOs have other colors, like brown, tan, pink, blue, and green. Newton's mom told him that he and Curie are "fraternal" twins, which is why they only kind of look alike. They were born at the same time, but Newton thinks that's about the only similarity.

Curie is quite the goody-two-shoes, and Newton is like "whatever". She loves being the teacher's pet. He does not like school. Newton doesn't understand why he dislikes school; he just knows he is not very good at it. He prefers sports and rough-housing. She prefers learning and reading, painting, or "anything boring," as he calls it.

Still, they get along pretty well, and look out for each other. Newton thinks it's just a thing twins do. She's a good sister, and for the most part, Newton is ok with having her around. It helps when you move around as much as they do. Newton's Dad one time told him that his job is to be something like an ambassador, so they have to move around a lot.

Newton cracks open the book and begins reading a few pages. It looks like a large cook book, like the one in Mom's kitchen. *Mom is nowhere NEAR a great cook,* Newton thinks. But he recalls that she does have a lot of cook books. Newton flips to a page and reads the top:

"Catapult" is the title. "To shift your shoebox into a catapult, you will need to learn basic physics. Specifically, how gravity works, Newton's laws, and kinematic physics…"

What? Newton stops a moment. His name is in the book? How bizarre. Well he certainly didn't make up any laws.

"My name is in this book," he says to Curie. Curie looks over at him, puzzled. "Uh, riiiiiiiight," she says.

"Can I see?" asks Dr. Braun.

"Yeah, sure," Newton replies.

He looks. "Ah yes, that is not you, Newton. That is a famous human scientist who taught us about force, but don't worry too much about that right now," he says.

Newton feels a bit let down and still puzzled. He watches Dr. Braun as the teacher continues talking and makes his way back to the front of the room.

"Newton has noticed a very interesting part of this class. Each section has instructions for how you can convert a shoebox into a useful tool."

"Why would I care to do that?" asks another TROBO in the class. Newton looks over. It's a larger TROBO. He's stronger, brown, and has a different chest emblem. It's a peanut. Newton looks down at his own chest to see an apple, and he sees Curie's atom symbol.

"What's your name, son?" Dr. Braun asks.

"Carver."

"Well, Carver, you may find it very helpful to have one tool when you are in one situation and a different tool when you are in a different situation. You might need a swing one time, a helicopter the next, and a submarine the next. Think of the shoebox as your very own Swiss Army knife with all sorts of abilities on demand," he says. "For example…"

Dr. Braun turns around and places something small on his desk. He presses a few buttons, and the desk begins to creak and moan. The legs lengthen. The desk divides into sections. Gears begin to turn. The desk quickly turns into a giant, mechanical mosquito. It rises up to the ceiling and buzzes its wings loudly. Its wings seem bigger than Newton's bed. The buzzing is so loud, it shakes the classroom windows. The whole class gasps. A few of the kids on the front rows dive out of their seats to get away from the long beak as it bends down to look for something tasty to eat.

Dr. Braun touches the little hexagonal gadget on the Mosquito's heel, and it transforms back into a desk.

Everyone is silent.

Some of the TROBOs are breathing heavy, and some start to giggle. One of them has peed his pants and asks to be excused.

"That was SO COOL!" one yells out, and the class erupts in chatter. Dr. Braun smiles at the stir he has created in the otherwise silent class.

"Now settle down everyone, settle down," he says calmly. They do.

A short, lavender TROBO raises her hand at the front of the room. "Yes, Emma," says Dr. Braun.

"I thought you said we'd be s'ape s'ifting s'oeboxes," she says in a very young voice with a lisp. Curie leans over and whispers, "I think she's a lot younger than us." He whispers back, "then why is she here?" Curie shrugs.

"Correct, Emma. I shape shifted a table, didn't I?" Dr. Braun replies. "I did that to show you we can shift other objects as well, but that's for very advanced users. Adults. We call them 'Comlok Masters'. You have to master many lessons and trainings before you can shift any object. I hope that inspires you. But in this class, you are shifting shoeboxes. When you go to HPS, you will learn to shift other objects."

"That's lame," Newton sighs under his breath.

"No, it's not, Newton," Dr. Braun calls out to Newton.
Newton is completely surprised. *How did he hear me,* Newton thinks.

"Learning to shape shift ANYTHING is terribly difficult, even a shoebox. You'll find out soon enough, that you have to study very hard to learn how to do it." He glares at Newton as if to say, "be

quiet until you know what you are talking about."
Newton is slightly uncomfortable.

Shape shifting shoeboxes comes from the ancient art
of Corugami. Corugami means "folding heavy
paper into any shape". It has taken centuries for us
to perfect this art, and so it pervades our culture.
That is why we named our school after it.

"In your books, are the instructions to make
whatever you dream up, but you are going to need
two VERY special things before you can do it."

The Library, Sort Of

The bell rings, and Dr. Braun doesn't finish his thought. "Ok everyone, onto your next class. It's down the hall and to the right," he calls.

"But what are the special things?" Curie asks. "You'll get there when you get there," he replies with a smile.

Newton and Curie grab their bags and head to the room down the hallway. As they walk, they catch up with Emma, the little purple TROBO. She's sucking her thumb.

"Wow, that's something only little kids do," Newton comments.

"Well then you better get th'tarted," she snaps back at him with a look of irritation.

"Alright, I like you already," he smiles.

"Wath's your name?" she asks.

"I'm Newton and this is Curie. And you're Emma. We heard the teacher say it," he replies.

"Yep, want to be friendth?" Emma replies. Still sucking.

"Sure," Curie says.

They walk on.

Everyone piles into the new room. This one is different than the last. There are no chairs. It's a

big circle with a hardwood floor. Newton thinks it feels more like a library. He hates libraries more than schools. The walls go up several floors in height, and there is a roll around ladder to get to all of the shelves.

They wait. Five or ten minutes go by after the bell rings.

"Well, I guess we can go," Newton starts to walk out.

"Hold on a minute there, physics boy!" yells a haggard voice from way up high. They all turn and look up. They can't see the person with the voice, and that's also when they realize the shelves go up. Waaaay up! Newton feels like the shelves go up much higher than the number of floors in the building. *Is that possible?* he asks himself.

"Wondering how many shelves are here? 113! Hah!" yells the voice from way up high. "Wait a second, I'll be right down!"

SQUEEEEEEEEEEEEEEEEEEEEEEEEEEEEEK The wheels screech as the rolling ladder spins around the room and the group of students.

SQUEEEEEEEEEEEEEEEEEEEEEEEEEEEEEE
EEEEEEEEEEEEEEEEEEEEEEEEEEEEEEEE
EEEEEEEEEEEEEEEEEEEEEEEEEEEEEEEE
EEEEEEEEEEEEEEEEEEEEEK!

It seems to take forever and the other kids are holding their ears by the time the voice gets to the ground to meet them. The voice is coming from a squirrely looking, old TROBO.

She stays on the ladder a moment, glaring above the students a few minutes, and then hops off. She has white hair and wrinkles where most TROBOs have skin. She has a toothless grin and a wild eyed stare.

Newton leans over to Curie, "does she scare you a bit?"

"Yeah." she replies.

"Everyone, I am Dr. Loch, and this is the comlok collection," she says. "Here you will pick your very own comlok. I'm in charge of..."

Curie raises her hand.

"Yes dear, what's your name?" Loch asks.

"I'm Curie. What's a comlok?" asks Curie.

Dr. Loch stopped a moment and turned to the class, asking "Yes class, who in here can tell our radiation friend, what a comlok is?"

Curie looks confused at being called a big word.

No one answers.

"Did Dr. Braun not get to it?" she asks. "Well that's ok. I'll try to pick up where he left off. The comlok is absolutely the most powerful tool you'll ever learn to control in your lifetime!"

"It will become your partner in creating things right out of your imagination. In a way, it is your super power." Having a super power seemed pretty neat to Newton.

She pulls a little black triangle about 4 or 5 inches wide off of the ladder, and the ladder transforms down into a small coffee mug. Bzzzt-Bop-Swizzz-Blip-Flap-Ding! It makes a series of gear, snapping, and flapping noises as it shrinks down.

She holds the triangle up proudly. Newton can see it has some numbers on it.

"This is a comlok!" she says. "When I type in a certain set of numbers, and press it onto an object, the object transforms into whatever I desire."

"That's what Dr. Braun had," Curie tells Newton.

"Yeah, but his is round," Newton replies.

"Yes, radiator," Loch says. "Comloks come in all different shapes and sizes, and you are here to choose yours."

The TROBOs start to look around at each other. They are excited at the idea of getting their own comlok. Even Newton is interested now.

"Ok, line up in a circle around the walls. I'll take each of you up on the ladder to choose your comlok," says Loch.

They all take their positions on the wall. Loch looks around the room and picks a tall, skinny TROBO. He is colored in browns and greens, and he has a paintbrush chest emblem. "You'll go first, art boy. What's your name?" she asks.

"I'm Dali," he replies in a foreign accent.

"Hello Dali," she laughs, "that's a film reference. Anyone know that film?" Loch looks around bemused.

Blank stares from everyone.

"Right. I'm old. Ok, here we go," she torts.

Loch places her triangular comlok on the coffee mug, and it snaps to it, like a magnet would to a refrigerator. She punches in a few numbers, and …
BZWEEEEE-TOOOOOOP-RRRRRRSSSRRRRRRRSRRRRRRSS-BLOOOOP-FIZZZZ - the coffee mug transforms back into the towering ladder. It looks a bit floppier to Newton this time. She pulls Dali onto the ladder, says, "Hang on", and they start spinning at a blurry speed. The wind picks up in the room, like a tornado.
"AAAAAAaaaayyyeeeeeeeeeeeeeeeeeee" comes from the ladder. Even though they have become blurry, Newton can tell Dali is scared and hanging on for dear life as they ride up the ladder rungs. Round and round they zoom.
"AAAaaaaayyyeeeeeeeeee" he continues until suddenly – THUD!
They stop. Loch and Dali are about 20 stories up and they are still.

Newton strains to hear them talk, but he can't. Then, as fast as they started, they begin spinning and zooming around the room.

"Aaayyoooooohoooohoooohooo," Dali screams out again.

They reach the bottom, and Dali steps off the ladder spinning in circles, weebling and wobbling. He lands on his tookus.

"Who's next?" Loch asks, looking around the room with a wild eyed grin. She clearly enjoys this part of her job.

Everyone is looking at Dali, waiting to watch him vomit on someone's shoes.

"You! Physics boy," she's staring right at Newton. "Hop on and don't be shy," she beckons him over. Newton looks around to see the whole class staring at him. *Talk about peer pressure,* he thinks.

He starts to move and eventually takes the bottom rung of the squeaky ladder.

BOOM! The ladder takes off, swirling around the room. The room becomes a blur, and Newton clamps on to his rung on the ladder, like it is the last thing he'll ever touch. The sound of the wind passing over his ears is like a windy microphone – FLUP FLUP FLUP FLUP... He looks up and can see Loch hanging on with one arm. She's using her hand to hold another cup of coffee. She's eating a cantuccini (a coffee biscuit) with the other. It's as if the ride doesn't even bother her. She smiles to him and winks as if to say, "This is fun, huh?"

He does not think fun is the right word.

The speed is just too much, and it seems like they've been going for a lot longer than Dali. His arms get weak. His legs, also wrapped around the ladder, are starting to slide. The dizziness takes over. His fingers start to slip. He can't hold on anymore, and Newton let's go!

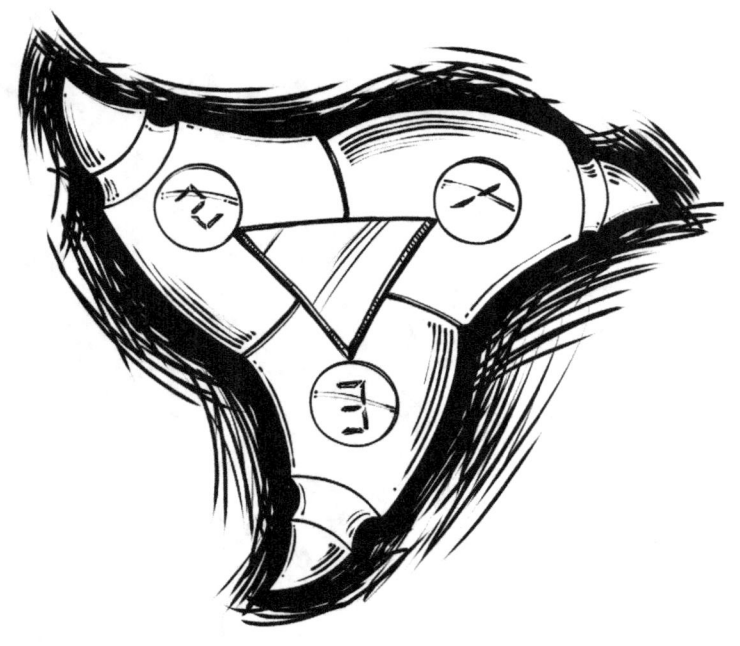

The Comlok

Newton feels himself start to fall. The ladder spins away. Loch is surprised. He starts to drop. For a moment, he feels weightless.

This must be like what the astronauts feel, he thinks.

A hand grabs his hand, and he stops falling. He looks to see it is Loch's. Newton, confused, looks at where she was a moment ago.

"Oh don't worry about falling, Physics boy. This ladder spins so fast, I zipped around and got you on the other side!" she yells above the loud wind.

"Hang on, we've got to stop soon!" she says.

"Why?" Newton calls out.

"Because we're --" she starts to say.

The ladder BOINGS to a stop, like a rubber band. They bounce back and forth a second.

"--at the top," she finishes. She blinks a moment. "I haven't been to the top of this thing in about 30 years," she says with a little surprise. Newton follows her gaze downward. He looks to the bottom of the ladder, but he can't see the ground. He just sees a black tube made by the stacks of circular shelves that surround them. The other TROBOs are so far away, he can't tell if they are even there anymore.

"Beautiful, huh?" Loch asks.

"Uh," Newton swallows back his vomit, "Yeah."

"Well here we are," she says.

Loch is smiling at a particular spot on a shelf. An object is lying there, and the lamp just above the object is glowing. The rest of the cherry stained, wooden shelves are dark.

"This is your comlok," she grins.

Newton gathers himself and he leans in. The object is kind of like a triangle, but more like a ninja throwing star. The three pieces of the triangle jut out like the legs of a starfish. On each leg is a number on something like a dial. Newton reaches his hand out to pick it up, and uses his thumb to roll the numbers on the dial. They go from zero to nine. It's surface is almost like glass. He holds it up and can see through the glass just a bit to the other side. In the middle is a triangular button made of shiny silver. He's mesmerized.

"Do you like it?" asks Loch.

"Yeah, it's uhm... cool," he replies.

"Thank you," she says and smiles.

Newton looks at Loch a bit confused.

"I made it," she goes on. "I make all the comloks," she smiles with a bit of pride.

"Wow, it must have taken you a long time to make all of these," he says.

"Yeah, forever," Loch smiles again.

"Well, in that case, I should thank YOU," Newton says.

"You're welcome, Newton. That happens to be one of my favorites," she smiles.

Newton is surprised. "How did you know my name?" he asked.

"Lucky guess," she winks. "Let's go!"

And with that, Loch kicks off the ladder in to motion with her foot. It spins, and they fly down the whirlwind of shelves in the same tornado style they used in coming up.

They get to the bottom, and Newton topples off like a bowling pin that just got slapped by a large bowling ball.

Curie comes over to ensure he's ok. He nods. All is well. The rest of the class get their comloks over the next hour.

Curie's comlock is oval and solid white like a piece of polished ivory. It has three numbered dials and a big gold button in the middle. She's very happy with it too.

Afterwards, the TROBOs go to other classes like Math, Agriculture, Drawing, Technology, and more. As the TROBOs go through the classes, Newton notices that each TROBO likes some and doesn't like others. In Math, they are told they will learn about basic math and will soon learn advanced stuff. In Agriculture, they start by discussing farm animals like pigs, horses, and chickens. In Drawing, they discuss how basic shapes like lines, circles, triangles, and rectangles can be used to draw anything. In Technology, they start by discussing how computers work. The day is long and they are both worn out by the time they get home.

Playing Hooky

Over night, Newton has some time to think about the school, the HPS thing, the shoeboxes, and comloks. It all feels very heavy. The next morning, Newton and his family start the whole routine all over.

Is it even real, he thinks. And if so, he feels the pressure of what all of it means. He rides in the back of Dad's car thinking things over. He decides it's not for him. It's way too much pressure. He just wants to have fun. So he makes a new plan - for the day at least.

After Dad drops Newton and Curie off, the class starts. Newton asks Dr. Braun for a hall pass to go to the restroom. "You should have gone before class started, Newton, but yes you can go," Dr. Braun snaps at him.

"Thanks," Newton replies and heads down the hall. He passes the boys bathroom and heads right outside. He keeps an eye out for teachers, ducking behind some bushes or cars as they come into work. Soon, he's made it to a park just a block away. Newton hopes to find some way to feel better about this new school. To feel better about learning how to transform stuff. To feel better about helping humans.

"I don't really even know what humans do. Why would I want to help them?" he asks out loud. No one answers.

He wants things to be simple again. He wishes there was a game of buckyball to play; he's good at that. But no kids are in the park, since it is a school day. He plays his pirates video game a while. He beats it again for the 50th time. He loves the cannons and the "argh mateys" and thinks of how cool it would be to be a pirate for a day. He imagines being a pirate for a while, slides, swings, and does everything the park has to offer. He walks the plank and fires a few fake cannons. He imagines being the captain of a huge crew. "You and you, cover the quarterdeck, you and you man the cannons, you and you protect the main deck, who's manning the rudder?" and on and on he goes, commanding his huge crew of imaginary pirates.

Newton hears a twig snap and out of the corner of his eye, he sees something black duck behind two bushes. This startles him, and he stops his pirate fantasy. He listens a moment. He sneaks towards the bushes, trying to see past the leaves. As he gets closer, a solid black robot that sort of looks like a TROBO jumps from the bushes and starts running away. Newton instinctively races after it, and calls, "Wait! Would you like to play?" But he soon realizes that the robot is really fast and doesn't want to play. He stops running. He huffs and puffs to catch his breath.

After a moment, he realizes it is getting late. He has gotten no new ideas for how to fix his school problem and decides it is a hopeless effort. He heads back to school.

Upon arrival, he sneaks back in, tip toes down the hallway, and hears Dr. Braun around the corner. "Ok, I'll look over here," Dr. Braun says to someone down the hall.

Newton steps into the bathroom and then comes right back out just in time to see Dr. Braun come around the corner. "Newton, there you are! Where have you been?"

"I uh, I was in the bathroom," Newton replies. He's not happy about lying, but he needs to save his skin. "Really? For two hours?" Dr. Braun asks. Dr. Braun looks at him very suspiciously waiting for Newton to slip up or confess.

"Yeah, I was …terribly sick. Stomach issues, y'know," Newton replies. As if on cue, his stomach makes a huge growl to make it more convincing. "Excuse me", he says.

Dr. Braun winces and looks him over once. There is silence.

"Right. Get back to class. You've missed some important lessons," he says.

They walk back to class, and Dr. Braun snatches the hall pass from Newton's hands.

On the ride home, Dad is on his cell phone talking with someone at work. "Something urgent has come up at work," he says. Curie is humming to herself a song they sang when they were children. Life seems good to her. Newton is looking out the window, sad and frustrated.

"Hey brother, everything ok?" Curie asks. Newton doesn't reply.

"Want to play bucky out in the yard tonight?" she pushes.

"Maybe," he replies.

"Where were you in class today? Is your tummy alright?" she asks.

"It's fine," Newton replies and glances over at Dad to see if he's listening. He's not.

"I was worried about you," Curie presses.

"I'm ok. It passed," Newton answers.

"You know, if you want to discuss--"

"I DON'T. I don't want to discuss anything. Just leave me alone will you?" he says to her in a harsh tone.

Curie is stunned and hurt. "Ok," she says and looks out the window. He immediately feels guilty, but he doesn't say anything else for the drive home.

That night, Newton's dad has a special talk with him after dinner. Dad takes a seat next to Newton on the floor where he's playing with some building blocks.

"Newt, let's talk," Dad says.

"Ok", Newton says, but he thinks, *Uh-oh.*

"What happened with school today, son?" Dad asks.

"What do you mean?" Newton replies, keeping his eyes to the floor.

"Newt, come on. Just be honest with me. Dr. Braun says you skipped out of shoebox class."

"Oh, well I was really sick and--"

"Newt", Dad interjects and tilts his head a bit to tell Newton the lie is not going to work here.

Newton thinks a moment.

"Yeah, I skipped out of class, I'm sorry," Newton replies.

"So what happened?" Dad pushes. Newton can tell Dad is not angry, but he does want to get the complete story. Dad is good about talking stuff out. "Dad, why am I at this school? I don't know why, but I'm not even supposed to BE in a magnet school. I don't even LIKE school, much less going to some place special. I'm not exceptional. I'm not even an egg head like Curie."

"Don't call your sister an egg head. She's just into school more than you are," Dad starts in.

Newton sighs.

"Ok wait, that's not the point," Dad starts again. "Son, how do you know you're bad at something until you try?" he asks. "How do you know you're not going to like this school? Curie told me they gave you your comloks yesterday. Wasn't that cool?"

"I don't know," Newton answers. Being young means you still don't have a way to express all your feelings.

"Newt, you never know what is inside you until you push yourself."

"It's a lot of pressure, Dad," he replies.

"I know son," Dad replies. "But I also believe you can handle it. I won't ask you to do something too hard for you to handle."

Newton doesn't feel like he is getting very far this time. "Ok, Dad."

"Will you give it a little more time?" Dad asks.

"Yeah."

"No more skipping?" Dad asks with a smile.

"No more skipping."

Dad gives him a hug and leaves. It isn't their best conversation, but Newton feels pleased that he's not getting punished for skipping - this time. But he gets the feeling that "punishment" is coming soon enough, even without Dad giving it to him.

Homework Stinks

Curie and Newton settle into class. They notice Dr. Braun is more excited than usual today.

"Kids, I'm thrilled to give you your first homework assignment!" he smiles.

The class grumbles.

"No, this is cool. Your homework is to make your shoebox transform into something simple," he continues.

Everyone looks around. Some smile. Some frown in dread. Curie smiles over at Newton. Newton frowns back.

"After yesterday's lesson, you now have all three pieces you need to shape-shift your shoebox," Dr. Braun goes on. "This Friday, you will demonstrate your homework to the entire class in a show and tell."

Newton gets nervous. He was not in class yesterday. He skipped. He recalls there are three things he must have to do this. One is the comlok. One is the "Shoebox Shape Shifting 101" book. He doesn't know what the missing third piece is. He looks over at Curie, who is beaming with excitement.

"Curie, what did you learn in class yesterday," Newton whispers to her. Curie looks over with confusion on her face.

"What?" she replies.

"What did you learn--"

"Newton!" Dr. Braun is talking to Newton now. "Please do no interrupt my instructions for homework. If you want to ask me something after class, you can do so then," Dr. Braun commands.

"Ok..." Newton replies quietly. Dr. Braun can be very scary sometimes.

Dr. Braun writes on the white board in giant letters, "WHAT IS SNOT?"

He looks back at the class. "Ok class, this is the beginning of your assignment. You must answer this question. This is a question many children ask when they are young. But just looking up the answer on the computer is too easy. Anybody can do that. It's also one of the humans' bad habits, but that's for another time. YOUR assignment is to use this question as *inspiration*! There are countless things you can do when discussing snot. What is it, where does it come from, why does it taste a certain way (the class says "ewww"), what causes it. You can go on and on," he says.

"Each of you must first learn as much as you can about snot and then on Friday make your shoebox transform into something related to snot," Dr. Braun announces.

"It should be tons of fun, and easy. Don't make anything too complicated for your first assignment," Dr. Braun says.

The bell rings, and they are all released to their next class. Everyone gets up to leave, and as Newton gets to the door, he hears Dr. Braun say, "Newton!"

Cringe.

He turns, "Yes sir?"

Dr. Braun looks at him for a moment with surprise and a little frustration, "Did you forget something?" Newton looks around in surprise, "Uhm... I don't think so."

Dr. Braun points to Newton's desk. Under it is a shoebox.

"That's your shoebox. Everyone else got theirs yesterday," Dr. Braun says.

"Oh," Newton replies and shuffles over to get it. As he leaves, he feels Dr. Braun watching him the entire way.

That night, Newton sits in his bed staring at the shoebox. He's bewildered. "I have no idea how to make this thing work. Am I already supposed to know this stuff? Dr. Braun didn't tell us how to do this," he complains.

He gets out his comlok out and stares at it. Dr. Braun got the table to shape-shift by putting his comlok on the table and punching in something. Loch got her coffee mug to turn into a ladder by putting her comlok on it and typing in something too. Newton looks over the dials on his comlok and decides to mimic them.

He puts the ninja star looking device on his shoebox. "SNAP!" It attaches itself to the shoebox much like a paperclip to a magnet. He spins the dials around. He puts a 2 on one dial, a 7 on another dial, and a 4 on the last dial. He steps back and waits for something to happen. Nothing does. He waits for a count of 10. Hmmm... nothing.

He reaches for the device and then all of a sudden, he hears a rumble in the walls, then a shake, and then a BOOM!!! He looks at the shoebox expecting to see something, anything, but it didn't move.

Then he hears Dad running down the hall screaming, "Honey! The sewage pipe just exploded. Call the plumber! I have to turn the water off!"

"Oh, I thought YOU made the boom," Newton says to the comlok. Disappointed, he goes to pick up the comlock, and it won't come off. It's stuck. He pulls at one side, and at another, and then trying to pry it off, his thumb presses the silver button. "CLICK!"

"WEEEE," the comlock starts to make a high pitched whirring sound. Gears start to click. Lines start coming out from all sides of the comlok and wrapping themselves around the box. Red lines. Blue lines. Green lines. Each tipped with a circle, triangle, or square.
Newton's eyes grow wide. Something is happening. He watches. The box edges begin to fold. Paper sounds like it is being torn. RRRRRIPPPP! Cards

being shuffled. FFFFFFFT-
SHTSHTSHTSHTSHTSHT-FFFFFT!

And then… "DOINK! WEUUURRRrrr..." the
comlok winds down. Gears grind to a halt. Lines
recede. And the whole thing folds back to the
shoebox with a "FFFFUUUURRTTT!!" sound.
Newton sees the shoebox return to normal and he
smells something. "Eww!" Cough cough! Smoke
comes out of the shoebox. It's corner starts to burn.
Newton smells rotten eggs, burning wood, and other
stinky smells all at once. The smoke fills his room.
The house fire alarm turns on, and Mom comes
running in.

"What is going on in here?" She opens the window,
taps out the fire, and tosses the smoking shoebox out
of the window.

"Are you ok?" she asks Newton.

"Yeah mom," he replies.

"Good. Now go outside and help your father. You two are causing more messes in 15 minutes than I've seen all week," she keeps fanning and motioning him to the door.

"Ok," Newton leaves to go outside.

Outside, Dad is talking to a plumber who just drove up. Newton takes a seat on the tree swing. Curie is on one of the branches reading a book.

"Hey," Newton says. She ignores him.

He knows she's still hurt from when he snapped at her in the car. "I'm sorry for being mean in the car," he says.

"You stink," she replies, never looking up.

"I know. I shouldn't have been mean--"

"No, I mean you smell like rotten eggs. What have you been doing?" she looks down with one eyebrow cocked at him.

"Oh," he replies, "I've been trying to make the shoebox transform."

She looks over to see the smoking shoebox on the ground outside their house. "Nice job."

"Yeah," he replies. "I don't know how to make it shape-shift."

"No duh," she shoots back.

They sit a moment in silence. Newton draws up some courage.

"Do you know how to do it? Do you think you could help me?" he asks.

"I thought you didn't want to discuss it," she says.

"No, I meant I didn't want to discuss why I skipped school yesterday," Newton replies.

"You skipped school?" her eyes widen.

Newton is surprised and a bit angry he let that part out.

"Uh yeah, but look, the point is, I'm not doing well with this new geek school, and I need some help. Will you help me?" asks Newton.

"Geek school?" Curie asks, a bit offended.

"Sorry, I didn't mean that YOU are a geek. I mean, this is not easy for me, but it seems like you are getting it. Is that true?" he asks.

"Yeah, I think so," Curie replies. She's getting it. She always gets the smart stuff. Curie knows she's faster at school stuff than Newton. But she likes to hear him say it from time to time.

Curie decides to help him. That apology is about as good as it will get from Newton.

"Yeah, I'll help you," she says.

She jumps off the branch. "So what have you tried so far," she asks.

Newton describes what he did in his first attempt to shift the shoebox.

"Oh I see, yeah you forgot the third part of the three things you'll need to shape shift anything," she replies. Taking a stance similar to Dr. Braun, she begins with a gruff voice, "First you need the shoebox, second you need the comlok, and last you need the most valuable thing – knowledge," she finishes with a finger in the air. She smiles waiting for Newton to compliment her perfect Dr. Braun impersonation.

Newton stares at her blankly. She gives up and uses her regular voice again.

"Look, yesterday in class, while you were out playing hooky, Dr. Braun said we have to learn the science and math behind how things work. If we want to shift the shoebox into a plant, we have to know the biology of that plant. If we want to transform it into a catapult, we have to know how catapults work. That includes the engineering *and* the physics. The comlok's ability to transform things is taken from our knowledge of the thing we are trying to create." She stops and waits.

"Oh… so it's not like a magic wand, where we whisper *hocus pocus* and we magically get what we want?" Newton asks.

"Nope," she says.

Newton's eyebrows drop, "So I still have to study?"

"Yep," she smiles.

He frowns. "Well that sounds hard. Isn't there an easier way?"

"Nope. Apparently as TROBOs, we have to know how to make things work. It's the only way we can teach the humans we help," Curie replies.

"I see. So what's next?" he asks.

Curies tosses the book she was reading to Newton.

"Read this. It's all about human snot," she grins.

"When you are done, I'll tell you how the numbers work."

"Numbers?"

Pop Pop Fizz Quiz

Newton is surrounded by doctors and nurses running frantically about. There is screaming and mumbling. Newton is in an emergency room, like the ones at the hospital. But it is also a barn with hay bales and chickens. Everyone seems confused. And then Newton sees why everyone is scared and running. There are pirates riding pigs around the emergency room chasing everyone. They are yelling, "gimme yer mucus, yarghh!!" Newton looks up and one pirate is coming right after him. "Why is he coming after me, I don't have mucus," Newton thinks. But then he feels his face. He has a nose? TROBOs don't have noses. His nose is gooey and green. He's sick and leaking snot out of his nose like a water hose. BUBBLE, BUBBLE, BUBBLE.

"What is going on?" he wonders. He turns and runs away from the scary pirate. Oops! Newton trips on a chicken in the emergency room and falls on his sticky face. He turns around to see the pirate jumping from a hay bale towards him with both hands reached out. The pirate yells, "BOOGERRRRRRRRRS!"

And Newton wakes up.

It was a dream. His heart is pounding. It's morning time, and he spent all night reading that snot book that Curie gave him. The snot book has doctors and hospitals in it. He feels his face for a nose. "Humans are gross," he says, wondering how he let the idea of snot be so revolting to him. Apparently it affected him so much, it oozed into his dreams.

Mom bangs on the door, "get up honey, time for school! You're gonna be late!"
Newton grabs a quick shower, a breakfast sandwich from the table and jumps in the car just as Dad is

cranking it up.   He tells Dad and Curie about his dream on the way to school.   It seems funny now. They get to school with a few seconds to spare.

"Welcome everyone, I have exciting news!" Dr. Braun says as he raises his hands to his side in triumph. Newton starts to dread the "exciting news" already.

"It's pop quiz time!" he yells with a little too much thrill in his voice.

"Pop quiz? What's that?" Newton thinks and looks over to Curie. She is beaming. Newton is not beaming.

"This quiz is on the snot book I gave you two days ago," Dr. Braun says. "Remember you need three things to make your shoeboxes work. First, the shoebox. Second, the comlok. Third, the knowledge of what you are trying to make." Dr. Braun begins handing out a sheet of paper with some questions on it. Newton's stomach gets queasy at the thought of the quiz.

"Let's see what you have all learned about snot," Dr. Braun smiles.

Newton has not finished the book. He tries his best anyways. His stomach gets no relief from taking the quiz. Curie zips right through the quiz, humming the entire time. Newton feels it is very distracting. "Shh!" Newton tells her. She looks back with a grimace and quits humming.

Newton turns in his quiz and asks to go to the bathroom. "Going anywhere else this time?" Dr. Braun asks with a look of disbelief.

"No," replies Newton. He doesn't look at Dr. Braun. He knows he deserved that remark.

After returning from the bathroom, Newton sees Dr. Braun is returning the quizzes, already with grades on them. Newton turns over the paper to read "F".

He failed it.

The bell rings. All the kids leave the room. Dr. Braun asks Newton to stay a moment. He does.

"What happened, Newton?" Dr. Braun asks.

"I didn't know I was supposed to read the book until last night. I got half way through it, but --"

"Stop," Dr. Braun says.

Newton is surprised and looks at Dr. Braun.

"Anyone can make excuses. Don't make them here," he stares at Newton. "If you don't want to be in this school, then don't be. If you want to be here, then prove it," Dr. Braun continues.

"Tomorrow is Shoe and Tell. If you apply yourself, you can catch up. If you apply excuses, you will fail." Dr. Braun lowers his voice and gets very close to Newton. "Let me say that a different way. If you don't shift your shoebox tomorrow, you will fail this class. If you fail this class, you will be asked to leave this school. I will not tolerate TROBOs skipping my class. I will not tolerate excuses either." He stares long and hard at Newton. Newton can't hold the stare back at Dr. Braun. He leaves the room feeling about six inches tall.

The Baby Sitter

Newton doesn't say much on the ride home. Curie asks him how the quiz went. He ignores the question. She knows from that, it did not go well.

Newton and Curie notice Dad is driving rather quickly to get home. "Dad, is everything ok?" Curie asks.

"Oh yes dear, I'm just hurrying, so your mom and I can make our airplane tonight."

"Airplane for what?" Curie asks. She's concerned. Dad is silent a moment and tilts his head as if he is surprised at something. "Uhm… our business trip. Didn't we tell you?"

"No" both Curie and Newton say.

"Oh, I think your mom was planning to tell you. It must have slipped her mind," he continues.

They get out of the car and Newton tries to pull his dad aside to discuss what Dr. Braun said earlier.

"Dad, can we talk a moment?" Newton asks.

Dad is walking fast into the house and up the stairs. "Son, I don't have a moment to lose. The airplane is leaving soon, and I see we haven't even packed everything." "Honey!" he calls out.

"But dad, I need your help with a homework assignment," Newton pushes.

"Oh sweetheart, I just don't have a moment right now. Can you ask your sister?" Dad replies.

Newton thinks of Curie, and he is angry with her for doing better at the quiz than he did. "No, she won't be able to help," Newton replies.

Just then, his mom comes out of their bedroom with suitcases, bags, and other travel gear all in a flurry.

"Oh there you are. Ready?" Dad asks Mom.

"Yep, let's move it!" she replies. She bends down, gives Newton a hug and then hugs Curie who walks up behind them.

"Wait, I really need help with my homework," Newton grabs his dad's pants leg. His Dad stops, turns, and squats to meet Newton eye-to-eye.

"Well then, you'll have to ask Grandpa," he says with a smile.

"Grandpa?" Newton asks in surprise.

"Yeah, he's gonna take care of you while we're gone," Dad grins a shaky grin.

Just then, from behind Curie and Newton, a thick cough rattles out from a grumpy old TROBO in a wheel chair squeaking up to meet them. He's grey, has a scruffy jaw, and says, "Hey kids, have you forgotten me already?" He holds out his hands for a big hug and a smell of mint floats their way. Newton's disappointment shows through his face. Curie stays quiet, with a bit of surprise on her face. "Uh, hi Grandpa," she says and looking first over to Mom and Dad, gives Grandpa a short hug.

"Hi," says Newton, who gives Grandpa an awkward pat on the knee. Grandpa TROBO and Mom and Dad exchanged a couple of quick glances and then Grandpa says, "Well, kids, let Mom and Dad go on their quick trip. They'll be back before you know it."

Newton and Curie give Mom and Dad hugs, and Newton says, "How long are you gone?"

"Just two nights. We'll be back before the weekend's over," Mom smiles.

"Grandpa's going to take good care of you," Dad says. And with that, Mom and Dad leave the house. Newton and Curie don't quite know what to say, so Grandpa jumps in first. "Don't worry about those two. Right now, we have more important things to worry about anyhow, like dinner!" He waves his hand and beckons them to follow him to the dining room. It is already laid out on the table, and they have a quiet meal.

After dinner, Newton and Curie clean up and then head outside. "So what's the deal with mom and dad up and leaving all the sudden?" Newton asks Curie.

"I don't know, but it's uncomfortable," says Curie.

"Why does *he* have to stay with us? We don't even see him except at the holidays once a year," Newton continued.

"I don't know," says Curie as she looks at the trees.

"And why do they think it is ok to leave us with just anyone," Newton asks.

"Well he *is* related to us, but beyond that, I don't know," replies Curie.

Newton feels even more frustrated with Curie's dumb answers.

"Do you know ANYTHING?" he grouches at her.

Curie is surprised at this attack. "Yeah, I know you still don't know how to transform your shoebox, and tomorrow's the big day. Are you going to keep yelling at me?" she looks at him angrily.

Newton gets silent when he's embarrassed.

"Whatever," he says.

"Fine," she says and goes in the house.

It's All In the Numbers

Newton is sitting in his room. The light is dark.

He's still angry. He stares at the shoebox. He

fiddles with the comlok.

Newton knows he has no chance now, but he's not going to let his know-it-all sister boss him. His pride is stronger than his will to go to this dumb school. "I didn't want to go there anyway," he grouches.

He looks out the window a moment. "I just need some help. Why do they all have to be so--" He thinks back to Dr. Braun's hassling him over the hall pass. He thinks about Dad rushing off to a business trip. That is so common and... frustrating. He taps the comlok on the window, agitated. He thinks back to Dr. Braun's remark from earlier today and repeats it in a mimicking voice, "If you don't shift your shoebox tomorrow, you will fail this class."

Newton doesn't want to fail. He thinks about the book. He thinks about the comlok. He thinks about the shoebox. He gets frustrated, because none of it makes sense. He jumps down from the window and kicks the shoebox into the hallway. "I just need some help!" he yells.

SQUEEK... SQUEEK... SQUEEK... A sound rolls down the hallway. A shuffling sound, and Grandpa TROBO appears in the doorway. In his wheelchair lap lies the shoebox. "Everything ok, Newton?"

Newton is embarrassed and turns way. Wipes his eyes.

"I heard somebody screaming a bunch about needing some help, so I thought I'd try to help," he goes on.

Newton doesn't reply, but he's listening. Grandpa sits a moment, listening too. They hear crickets outside.

"I know we don't know each other that well, Newton, but that could change. With a little bit of work from you and a little from me, I bet we could become pretty good friends. Perhaps I could even visit more often."

Newton listens.

"But that's a different issue. For now, I think we have a more urgent problem to solve. I'd swear I heard someone say something about failing a class." Grandpa rolls in a few feet further, parks himself next to Newton's half bunk bed.

Newton's eyes widen. Grandpa heard everything!

"We can't let that happen. Especially when it is so easy to shape shift shoeboxes."

Newton turns. His face is full of surprise.

"What, you think you kids are the only ones who learn how to transform a box into an airplane?" Grandpa says, smiling like he's just won two free movie tickets.

"I uh, don't understand," Newton replies.

"Look here, grandson. Grandpa was once young like you. And I learned a few things along the way. How's about you let me help you on this one, and we'll see how it goes?"

Newton thinks a moment. *Well… what have I got to lose?*

"Ok, sure," Newton brightens up.

"The key to operating your comlok is the numbers," Grandpa begins. "Once you know the science and math of how something works, you place your finger on the dials. One number is for math. One is for science. The numbers will find themselves for you. If you don't know the science and math, the numbers will be wrong, or they'll spin forever. And if you try to fake the numbers, you could blow the box up." Grandpa taps the burn marks as he says this, and Newton raises his eyebrows. "oh."

"How do I know I got the right numbers," Newton asks.

"You'll know," Grandpa replies. "Show me your comlok."

Newton lifts up the ninja star, and Grandpa motions to him to put it on the shoebox.

"Next, what are you trying to build?" Grandpa says.

"What do you mean?" Newton replies.

"Well, you have to know what you want to build before you can transform the shoebox," Grandpa explains. "A tractor, a car, a laser beam, a mechanical goat, whatever. You have to focus your attention on that object, when you program the comlok."

"Oh, well we're studying snot," Newton replies.

Grandpa thinks a moment. "You can't really make it into snot. You have to convert it into something with structure, not a pile of goo," he says,

"OK, so this snot homework... what thing related to snot do you want to make?" Grandpa asks.

"Well, I don't know" Newton replies. "I know a lot more about snot after reading the book, but that doesn't mean I know what to make for tomorrow."

"Well take a second, close your eyes. What about snot inspires you?" Grandpa urges.

Newton winces a moment. Maybe grandpa is just a bit too kooky in his old age. "Why would snot inspire anything?" he asks.

"Come on," Grandpa tilts his head and raises an eyebrow, "Just try."

Newton closes his eyes. They wait. Newton's mind stays blank. He starts to get frustrated again. He opens his eyes. "I'm not getting anything. Look Grandpa, I'm not smart like Curie. I don't like to study. I don't know lots of science and math. I don't even like school. They expect way too much of you there. I'm too dumb. I don't belong in that school!"

He runs over to the window again. He hides his eyes. They are quiet a moment.

"Well I've certainly heard that one before," Grandpa chuckles. Newton is surprised at his laughter. "Y'know, you and your dad get more alike every year. That's a compliment, by the way."

Newton turns back to see Grandpa smiling. "Your dad wasn't super smart in school either. He certainly wasn't the teacher's pet. More like the teacher's scourge. But he did have something very special about him. Actually I should say *does* have something special about him. And you do too."

Newton looks at him confused.

"Magnes told me about your dream from the other morning – the one with all the snot, the emergency room, and pirates," Grandpa smiles.

Newton nods.

"That's *imagination*, my boy!"

Newton is still confused.

"*That* is the third number on the comlok!" and he points to the ninja star looking object Newton left on the shoebox.

"The powerful part of being a TROBO, especially one that is being trained for HPS, is that you don't have to be good at *every* thing. You have to be good at *some* thing. You have to be VERY good at something" Grandpa continues.

"And you have a GREAT imagination Newton," Grandpa presses.

Newton is beaming and feels redeemed.

"Graaaaandpaaa, I need your help with my computerrrr" yells Curie from down the hall. Grandpa turns to hear her.

"Ok, Newt, I'll leave you with this thought. Close your eyes one more time, and imagine something that really excites you. Something that inspires you. Something that you KNOW ALL ABOUT. When you get that in your mind, the snot part will come. Ok?" He asks.

"Ok Grandpa," Newton smiles.

Grandpa smiles, puts the box and comlok on Newton's dresser and wheels out.

"Grandpa?" Newton asks.

"Yes?" Grandpa stops a moment.

"Can you tell me more about Dad when he was a kid sometime?" he asks.

"You bet," Grandpa winks and rolls out of the doorway.

By Rhino, I Think I've Got It!

"Grandpa is right," Newton thinks. "I'm good at stuff. I don't have to be a brain to be good at stuff. I can do this. I'm as good as any of those other students. I'm as good as Curie. I just have to focus my mind. My imagination…"

Newton closes his eyes. He thinks about anything. He thinks about everything. His thoughts are flooded with the events of this past week. He pushes back the angry thoughts. He thinks about the school. He thinks about his mom. His dad. He thinks about the other kids in the school. He thinks about snot. He thinks about Loch. What did she say? He thinks about spinning around on that crazy ladder. He thinks about his dream in the emergency room. He thinks about the doctors and nurses running. He thinks about snot being everywhere. He thinks about the pirates. He thinks about playing hooky. He thinks about jumping up and down on the playground swings and jungle gyms. He thinks about playing pirate on them, saying 'yargh' and firing cannons. He thinks about Dr. Braun's giant mosquito. He thinks about snot. He thinks about pirates… He thinks about… He thinks about…

"I've got it!"

Newton has found his idea. His first idea. He opens his eyes. His heart is pounding. His palms are sweaty. He's got it.

He grabs the shoebox. He grabs the comlok. He goes to the window opens and breathes the fresh air. "It's going to be awesome," he says.

He stares out the window until he calms down. And places them next to himself in the bed. For the first time all week, Newton finally knows how he's going to prove himself worthy of the school. He's going to prove to Dr. Braun, and to himself, he can do this.

Newton goes to sleep, smiling.

Shoe and Tell

That morning in class, everyone is buzzing about
their shape-shifting shoebox ideas. "Shoe and Tell"
promises to be exciting for everyone, although
nervous energy is also high in the room.

"Ok everyone, are you ready to show us an object you have created to help explain snot to children?" Dr. Braun asks the room. He gets a series of nods and stares from the room.

"Great, let's get right to it then!" he says and blows his air horn

BREEEEEEEEEEEEEEEEEEEEEEEEP!

First up is Dali. Newton recalls he's a bit of an artist from his paintbrush chest logo, so it comes as a surprise when Dali unveils his shoebox shifted into a large microscope. He excitedly shows a few plates with different bacteria in the microscope to Dr. Braun. Dali proudly talks about each slide, "… and this one is the Rhinovirus. It causes the common cold. The Latin word for nose is *rhin*, like a rhino."

"Very impressive, Dali, well done!" Dr. Braun says.

Up next is Emma. She pulls a drape off of her shoebox, which has been transformed into a set of about 40 giant arrows on coils. She pushes a big red button, and the arrows spring around the room, pointing to all sorts of spots where cold germs could be hiding. "They can be on thi'th door knob, that th'eat, that marker, this th'tapler, your handths, your fathe, thi'th bottle of water, the bathroom patheth…" Emma goes on and on. Newton can tell other TROBOs are starting to get freaked out. Even he feels an overwhelming need to go wash his hands.

"Ok thank you Emma, that was very … thorough," Dr. Braun stops her. "Great attention to detail, and nice work on the shape-shifting."

Emma smiles and skips back to her seat.

A few more students go, and then it is Newton's turn.

"Newton, where is your Shoe and Tell?'

"Oh I have it here," pulls out his box and comlok.

"It's not transformed?"

"Uh no, I thought I was… supposed to transform it in class," Newton replies.

"But you *have* already transformed it once, right?" Dr. Braun presses.

Newton realizes yet another detail he missed. "Uh no," Newton gets nervous. He looks over at Curie who is clearly concerned for her brother. Her toes twist in a bit.

Dr. Braun blinks in surprise. "Well, this ought to be good," he huffs.

Newton looks back at him. He is very uncomfortable now. He was so excited, he had not considered that he might fail.

"Well, get on with it!" Dr. Braun snaps at him. Newton puts the box on the floor. His mouth feels dry. He pulls out his comlok. He presses it to the box, and it snaps on like a magnet. Just like the other night.

He remembers the object he wants to transform the shoebox into. He touches his finger to the first dial. The science dial. It spins and locks in a number. He touches the second dial. The math dial. It spins and locks in a number. Newton feels like this is going well. He knows the science. He knows the math. Now for the imagination. He presses the third dial. The number spins. The number spins. It's not locking. The number spins. Newton looks up at the class. The number spins. He notices his classmates are looking at him awkwardly. "Why is it taking so long," he wonders. The number spins. He looks at Curie. She is tapping her feet nervously. The number spins. Newton starts to worry. He starts to forget his idea. *I'm not smart enough* creeps in. The number spins. *I can't do this,* he hears his own voice in his head. He looks around the room. The number spins.

He locks eyes with Dr. Braun. Dr. Braun's eyes narrow. They seem to say, "I knew it."

The Snot Shot

Newton's eyes narrow. He thinks of his Grandpa's words. "I'm not going to let you make me feel like a failure. I'm stronger," Newton thinks. He closes his eyes. He imagines his object. He sees it growing, glowing majestically, and spewing snot out of all sides like a glorious fountain of gooey mucus.

CLICK... The number stops.

Newton opens his eyes. He looks at it. He looks at Dr. Braun. He smiles and presses the silver button. Dr. Braun's eyes widen.

The ninja star shaped comlok begins to hum. Newton can feel it getting warmer. Colored lines extend from all sides, wrapping themselves around the shoebox. The lines draw circles, triangles, and squares at special positions all around the shoebox. Newton watches as what looks like a diagram of what will be built is drawn on top of the shoebox. Where circles are drawn, gears and other round shapes extrude out of the box. Squares cause flaps and other hinges to fold out from the box. Triangles cause other flaps and extrusions to come out of the box. The box then begins to flip and fold along the diagram lines just drawn.

BZZZZZ, RRRRRRRIP, FRRRRRRRRRP, ZZZZZZT, KIKIKIKIKIKIKIKIKI, TRRRRRRRR,

The shoebox makes all sorts of gear noises and paper tearing noises as it transforms. Newton thinks he hears shuffling of cards and Velcro tearing open.

MNNNNNNNN, BPPPPPPPPP, RRRRRRRIIPP, BZZZZZZZZZ, TKTKTKTKTKTKTKTKT, KCHING, KCHING, ZZZZWEEEEEEEEPPP

Out from the tiny little shoebox extends an array of pieces, flaps and sides, until what was a shoebox has now folded, torn, and otherwise transformed itself into what looks like a giant…

"Pig nose?" Dr. Braun says. "Is that a pig nose?" he asks with a large confused look on his face.   The class is silent.

"Actually, it's a snot cannon!" Newton announces proudly.

"A snot… cannon," Dr. Braun repeats with a look of concern. Someone giggles.

"Yeah a snot cannon!" Newton repeats. Then he unrolls a bull's eye poster and starts taping it to the other side of the wall.

"What are you doing, son?" Dr. Braun says.

"I'm going to show you what happens when snot is ejected from a nose!" he smiles. "But instead of it being a completely random spray, I decided kids would have more fun, if they could shoot the snot, like pirates used to shoot their cannons back on their ships." Newton finishes taping up his target, runs over to the giant pig nose cannon and strikes a match.

"*Wait, wait*, wait, wait, wait," Dr. Braun stops him. "You can't go shooting a cannon in a school building!"

"But it's just snot," Newton replies.

"No I'm sorry Newton, that's against *some* safety regulations somewhere, I'm sure," Dr. Braun says.

"But I won't be able to show you what it can do," Newton presses.

"You won't have to. I get the idea. I'll figure out what grade to give you without you demonstrating the cannon," Dr. Braun says. "Go back to your seat please, Newton." Newton is speechless. He blows out the match. He hangs his head and goes to his seat. He doesn't make eye contact with Curie.

"Next! Who's next?" Dr. Braun pushes the pig nose cannon to the side and looks at his list of students. "Carver, come on up."

Newton watches as Carver goes up to the front. He can tell Carver is nervous. "Germs are n-not the only things that cause animals to make snot." Pollen can also cause them to make snot by triggering allergies. He unveils his shoebox transformed into what Newton could only describe as a large mechanical sunflower in a pot.

The class oohs and ahhs, and the sunflower is quite beautiful, and they are all a bit surprised to see something that looks so organic come from a shoebox.

"That's nice work, Carver, thank you. I can see your interest in botany really coming through here," Dr. Braun says. Carver gains some confidence, but he's still nervous.

"It's cooler than that, Dr. Braun. I-I m-made it a working flower," he smiles and presses something on the back. The flower begins to shake just a little, the head lunges back and forth in a rhythmic motion, and then Newton, Curie, and the other students see a fine yellow dust is coming off the middle of the flower. Pollen.

"It's making pollen!" Carver says triumphantly.

"Huh, well that is extremely creative, well done Carver," Dr. Braun smiles and writes down something in his book. "You can turn it off now." Carver smiles big and presses something on the back of the flower, but it doesn't stop. The pollinating flower keeps puffing out pollen. Carver arches his eyebrow.

Dr. Braun looks up from his notes and repeats, "Turn it off, Carver".

Carver taps the button again, and looks more confused. It starts shaking, pumping twice as fast.

It clouds up a puff of yellow dust. The room gets hazy. A couple TROBOs are coughing.

"It's broken s-sir," Carver nervously looks at Dr. Braun, who smacks his forehead and says, "Why me?" He gets up to have a look.

Newton notices something beginning to wiggle a little beside Carver. It's his pig-nosed snot cannon.

SNORT! SNORT! SNORT!

He sees it's sniffling. It's reacting to the pollen.

Uh oh, Newton thinks and runs over to move it, but he's too late.

SNORT SNOOOOO-BLAM-SQUIRT!!! SN-BLAM-SPACK!!! SN-BLAM-SPLOCH!!!!

The nose cannon is firing huge, head-sized snot balls around the room, spinning after each fire.

"Run!!" yells Carver as he dives under a desk, just getting missed by a huge lugee-ball. The ball instead lands smack-dab into Emma's lap.

"Ewww!!!" she screams.

SNORT-BLAM-SLKAKK!

For a moment, Newton imagines the cannon and the pollinating flower are teaming up to cover the entire room in phlegm. Newton chuckles a bit, but he realizes he's got to do something. He runs up to the back of the pig nose cannon, which spins around and plasters him flat against the wall.

It knocks him out a second, and things go quiet. Then it all comes rushing back at him, and Newton realizes his last week has just flashed before his eyes.

He sees Dr. Braun wiping off the biggest pile of green gooze yet and hears him screaming at him again, "NEWTON!! Wake up!! Turn off your cannon!" Dr. Braun makes a run for the cannon, but it swings around and hits him in the head. He's knocked to the ground, unconscious.

Newton shakes his head to clear it up. Looks around to see everyone hiding under their tables now. Several of the other students have made it out into the hallway, but there are a few left. "The room is under attack!" he thinks.

Then it clicks. He, the mighty pirate captain, forms a plan. "Everyone, I'm gonna need some help! Here's what we need to do!" he screams as he peels himself off the wall and lands on his butt with a THUD. "Emma and Dali, grab the flower. Push it out of the room!"

"Carver, ever play buckyball? Double-team the cannon. You tackle low, I tackle high," he calls. Carver nods.

"Curie, when the nose is done, come help us," he calls to his sister.

"Everyone, on the count of three! One... Two... Three... GO!!" Newton screams. The room moves into slippery action. First Dali and Emma swish swash their way over to the great shaking flower. It keeps pumping out the pollen powder. And as if the nose cannon were aware of the plan, it spins around and SPLATTERS both of them with double-sneezy goo bombs.

SNOR-BLAM-SPLICKYT! SNORT-BOOM-SCUT!!

They stumble, but continue to push the writhing sunflower out of the room, nearly slipping on the green gooze on the floor. They make it!

"Go Carver, go!" Newton calls, and Carver scurries to his feet, takes a couple steps, and leaps low into the air wrapping his arms and face around the wheel of the cannon. Newton runs in, trying not to fall, and dives for the top of the cannon. Together they flip the thing on its back. It's firing up to the ceiling and spraying down on them with a fountain of green goop. SNORT-SPLOOK! SNORT-SPLACK. It still convulses back and forth causing Newton and Carver to have to hang on to it like they are wrangling a large bull.

Curies comes over, "Now what?" she asks. "Jump on top and squeeze its nose," Newton calls.

"What?" she asks with surprise.

"Remember in the book? One way to stop people from sneezing is to squeeze their nose," he insists.

"Oh, yeah, but another way is to shine a light in their eyes," Curie says. She's not excited about squeezing a big gooey nose, and until now she's avoided getting shot.

SNORT-SPLACK!! SNORT-CHA-PLOOK!!

She dodges it.

"It doesn't HAVE eyes, Cur!" Newton screams.

"Oh right, ok fine," she says, looks at the wrestling match and jumps! She grabs a nostril. It sneezes. She grabs another nostril and tries to pull them together.

It sneezes. She squeezes. It sneezes. She squeezes. It sneezes again, and again, and then finally... it stops. Curie is covered head to ankle in gooey snot. She breathes heavily. Newton and Carver breathe heavily. The cannon has stopped firing. They all let go and lay on the floor exhausted. Newton is giggling just a bit, and the other two look at him like he is nuts.

"Yarrgh," he smiles.

The door to the classroom opens, and the others come back in. Newton and the others wake up Dr.

Braun. In comes the principal, "What is all the ruckus? Oh gross. What is all this snot?" she asks. Dr. Braun shakes his head and says he'll explain everything. "But first," he says, "Curie, I think we can do with your Shoe and Tell, now."

Curie wipes the snot off her face and smiles. She unveils her transformed shoebox, which is sitting in the back of the room. It is a large bundle of arms with gears and winches connected to a bunch of hands with handkerchiefs. "I decided a handy invention in an emergency room would be a machine that could wipe 100 noses at once. But perhaps it will work just as well right here," she says and shifts a gear. The 100-handed wiping machine hums into action.

BZZT, KZZT, FTTTTT, BEEEP, BUUUURT, ZZZEEEP, KZIPPP--

Hands with handkerchiefs begin wiping in all directions. TROBOs get wiped down, walls get wiped, ceilings get wiped, the pig-nosed cannon gets wiped. After about 15 minutes, all of the green goop has been wiped up and into a large trash can. The room is still a little sticky and stinky, but the worst is all gone.

"Class is dismissed for today, kids. Go home and ...shower," the principal announces with a grimace. She and Dr. Braun walk down the hallway as he fills her in on the details.

Making the Grade

That next morning, Mom and Dad get home from their trip. Mom is already in the kitchen, and Dad is bringing in the suitcases, as Newton and Curie come running down stairs to greet them. The little TROBOs hug Dad. Both Newton and Curie are smiling ear to ear.

"Well, how were your past couple of days, kids?" Dad asks. "Great!" says Curie.

"Interesting," says Newton.

"Ok, what does that mean for each of you?" Dad asks.

"We got back our grade for our first Shoe and Tell, Dad, and I got an A!" Curie hoots as she is nearly bouncing out of her chair.

"That's terrific honey," and he reaches up for a high five. Curie slaps it happily. Dad looks over to Newton. Dad can tell Newton might have bad news.

"Curie, why don't you go show Mom your A," he encourages her. Curie runs happily squealing to the kitchen.

"Well, Newt, how did it go?" Dad asks him kindly. Newton looks up at the top of the stairs. He sees Grandpa rolling out of his room near the banister. He smiles down at Newton.

Newton smiles, "It's ok, Dad, I got a C."
"Alright, son!" Dad goes for another high five and Newton slaps it.
"Dr. Braun said although I got my shoebox transformed, I could have chosen an easier way to make snot, than with a cannon."
"Snot? With a cannon?" Dad asks and looks up concerned at Grandpa. Grandpa shrugs.
"I'll tell you all about it over breakfast," Newton says.

Dad smiles, "I'm looking forward to it." He stands up and says, "Let's go tell your mother." After a moment, Dad asks "So you think things are gonna be ok?"

Newton nods, "Yeah, I guess Corugami won't be so bad after all. I just needed to find my gift."

About TROBOs

TROBOs are named after humans who have done something important in science, technology, engineering, art, or math. We won't tell you who it is, but if you research, you are sure to find out the person after whom each TROBO is named. Have a look below to meet our heroes!

TROBO: Newton

Specialty: Physics

Favorite Color: Primary Red

TROBO: Curie

Specialty: Chemistry

Favorite Color: Purple

TROBO: Emma

Specialty: Math

Favorite Color: Pale Yellow

TROBO: Carver

Specialty: Botany

Favorite Color: Peanut Tan

TROBO: Dali

Specialty: Art

Favorite Color: Olive Green

Thank You

Thank you for making this book better for everyone:

The Chrisman family

The Wasserman family

The Elliot family

The Scheinberg family

Steve Alcorn

Megan Meehan

Alan Jordan

Asher Harden

www.ingramcontent.com/pod-product-compliance
Lightning Source LLC
Chambersburg PA
CBHW060440130626
46555CB00005B/2446